It's Okay to Be Different

Todd PARR

Megan Tingley Books

LITTLE, BROWN AND COMPANY

New York ✦ Boston

To Megan
for believing in something different

Love,
Todd

Little, Brown and Company

Hachette Book Group
1290 Avenue of the Americas, New York, NY 10104
Visit our website at www.lb-kids.com

Little, Brown and Company is a division of Hachette Book Group, Inc.
The Little, Brown name and logo are trademarks of Hachette Book Group, Inc.

The publisher is not responsible for websites (or their content) that are not owned by the publisher.

First Paperback Edition: April 2009
Originally published in hardcover in September 2001 by Little, Brown and Company

Library of Congress Cataloging-in-Publication Data

Parr, Todd.
  It's okay to be different / by Todd Parr.—1st ed.
    p. cm.
"Megan Tingley Books."
Summary: Illustrations and brief text describe all kinds of differences that are "okay," such as "It's okay to be a different color," "It's okay to need some help," "It's okay to be adopted," and "It's okay to have a different nose."
  [1. Self Esteem—Fiction.]   [2. Individuality—Fiction.]   I. Title
PZ7.P2447 It 2001
[E]—dc21   00-042829
ISBN: 978-0-316-04347-2 (PB) / ISBN 978-0-316-66603-9 (HC 10x10) / ISBN 978-0-316-15562-5 (HC 9x9)

10 9

IM

Printed in China

It's okay to be missing a tooth (or two or three)

It's okay to have a different nose

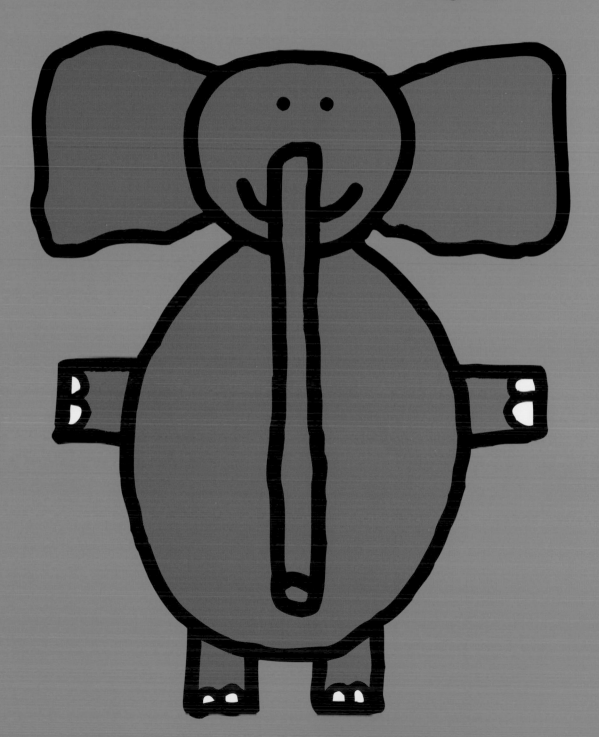

It's okay to be a different color

It's okay to have

no hair

It's okay to have BIG ears

It's okay to have wheels

It's okay to be

Small   Medium

Large   Extra Large

It's okay to eat
macaroni and cheese
in the bathtub

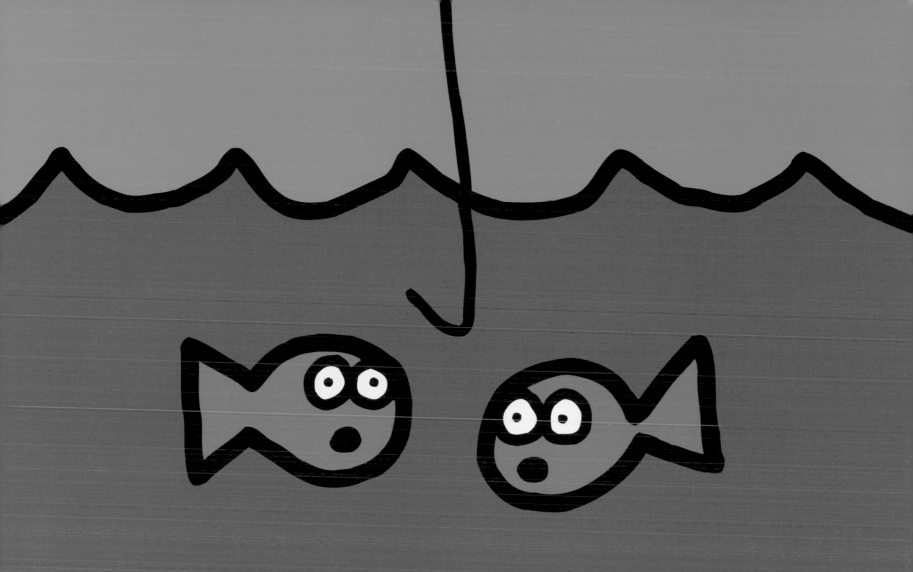

It's okay to say NO
to bad things

It's okay to come
from a different place

It's okay to have a pet worm

It's okay to be
proud of yourself

It's okay to have different
Moms

It's okay to have different
Dads

It's okay to have an invisible friend

It's okay to do something nice for someone

It's okay to get mad

I 's okay o help a
squirrel collect nuts

It's okay to have different kinds of friends

It's Okay to be different. You are special and important just because of being who you are.

Love,
Todd